Might goes hand in hand with right as He-Man and the Masters of the Universe fight to make their planet safe. The greatest of their enemies is Skeletor, the Lord of Destruction, and his evil band, whose hatred for their foes is never-ending. The war goes on but who will win?

First edition

© LADYBIRD BOOKS LTD MCMLXXXIV and MATTEL INC MCMLXXXIV

Wings of Doom

by John Grant
illustrated by Robin Davies

Ladybird Books Loughborough

High among the peaks of the Mystic
Mountains lay the beautiful land of Avion. The
people of Avion had the power of flight, and the
most skilled of all in the air was their leader,
Stratos. Stratos had many times helped He-Man
and his friends in their fight against evil. And
because of this he had made a deadly enemy of
Skeletor, Lord of Destruction. At length Skeletor
decided to punish Stratos. He knew, however,

that Stratos was clever and brave. Only by a trick could the Lord of the Air be lured into Skeletor's clutches.

Skeletor knew that Stratos had a lovely wife called Delora. If she were in danger, nothing would stop Stratos coming to her aid. Too late, Stratos would discover that he had walked into a trap.

Skeletor called for one of his slaves and gave him instructions for the kidnapping of Delora.

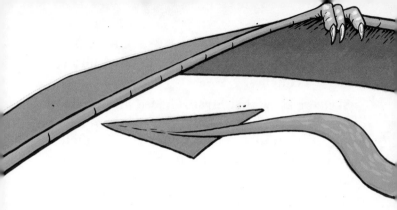

In the warm early morning sunshine, Delora stood on the balcony of her home. Far below lay the peaceful Avion countryside. Suddenly a speck appeared in the sky. High above the mountain peaks it grew steadily bigger. Was it a messenger seeking Stratos?

Delora strained her eyes to see. Too late she realised that it was not one of Stratos' people. It was not even human. It was a giant winged reptile, a wyvern, one of the evil creatures in the service of Skeletor, Lord of Destruction.

The wyvern circled above the house, its long neck swaying from side to side as it searched for its prey. Then, with a loud screech the winged monster swooped down in a powerful dive. Delora ran for the door leading into the building. The wyvern sailed across the balcony, seized her in its talons, and in a moment was winging its way back across the mountains before she could utter a single cry.

High in the chill air the wyvern soared. Soon
the Mystic Mountains lay far behind. Ahead,
grey snow clouds showed where the Ice
Mountains towered above the bleak northern
lands of Eternia.

A gap appeared in the snow clouds. The
wyvern with its burden made for the gap, and
Delora felt a gust of warm air. But the air was
foul and evil-smelling. It rose from the surface
of a volcanic lake which boiled and bubbled far
below. The snow-covered mountains surrounded
the lake. A barren island lay in its centre. On

the crags surrounding the lake scores of wyverns perched, their leathery wings folded. They were the fierce sentinels of the lake.

The wyvern carrying Delora glided over the island and put her down on the gravel shore.

In Snake Mountain, Skeletor rubbed his hands with satisfaction as he sent a message to Stratos:

"YOUR WIFE WILL BE RETURNED SAFELY TO AVION IF YOU SURRENDER YOURSELF INTO MY POWER."

Stratos was with his friends, He-Man, Teela and Man-at-Arms in Castle Grayskull when he received Skeletor's message.

"I must go to Snake Mountain immediately!" he cried. "There's no knowing what might happen to Delora if I do not agree to Skeletor's terms!"

"No," said He-Man. "We cannot trust Skeletor to free Delora even if you do give yourself up. That way we shall achieve nothing. We must match cunning with cunning. Our first task is to discover where Delora is held prisoner. We shall meet here again tomorrow. Before then I hope that I will have learned more of Skeletor's evil plot."

Leaving the castle on Battle-Cat, He-Man set off at speed for the royal palace of Eternia.

In a grove of trees close to the palace he dismounted, and became Prince Adam. With Battle-Cat also transformed into the cowardly Cringer he strolled through the gates.

As gentle Prince Adam, He-Man lost no time working out a rescue plan. In the top-most turret of the royal palace were stored ancient books and maps. In them was all the knowledge and wisdom of the Kingdom of Eternia. Here was perhaps a clue to Skeletor's hiding place for his prisoner. Only a creature of the air could have snatched Delora from her balcony. Skeletor had many evil winged things at his command. Griffins, harpies and wyverns were the biggest and most powerful. But they all lived within the depths of the Evergreen Forest, far from Avion.

In an ancient scroll there were pictures of wyverns. They were perched among the crags of the Ice Mountains. Was that where Delora was held prisoner?

At that moment a shadow fell on the scroll. At the open window hovered a giant falcon. It was Zoar, messenger of the Sorceress.

In his mind Prince Adam heard the voice of the Sorceress:

"DELORA IS GUARDED BY EVIL WYVERNS IN THE VALE OF CALDOR."

Prince Adam looked again at the scroll. Now he saw that it was a sort of map. And in the centre of the mountains was a spot marked: The Vale of Caldor. It lay many miles to the north. There was not a moment to lose. He turned to the window, but Zoar had gone.

Hurrying from the turret with the scroll, Prince Adam went to his private chamber. Holding high the Sword of Power he cried:

"BY THE POWER OF GRAYSKULL!"

And a moment later he was speeding towards Castle Grayskull as He-Man.

In the council chamber of the castle, He-Man showed his friends the ancient scroll and told them of the Sorceress' message. Quickly a plan was made.

In order to draw Skeletor's attention, Stratos agreed to pretend to surrender to the Lord of Destruction. Meantime, He-Man, Teela and Man-at-Arms would travel in the wind raider to the Ice Mountains on a rescue mission.

As the Masters of the Universe were about to
set out, Stratos handed He-Man a ring. "There
are only two of these rings on the planet," he
said. "Delora has the other. They glow in each
other's presence and will help you to find her."

And while Stratos flew off towards Snake
Mountain and the lair of Skeletor, He-Man set
the wind raider on course for the Ice Mountains.

As they landed on the foothills He-Man said,
"The wind raider will find it difficult to cross
those peaks with a full load. We must seek a
pass or some other route to the Vale of Caldor."

As he spoke, a voice rang out and a figure
appeared on a high rock.

"HALT! WHO TRAVELS IN THESE HILLS?
DO YOU COME AS FRIENDS OR ENEMIES?"

"That is one of the dwarfs," said Man-at-Arms. "They are good friends of mine. They mine much of the rare metal I need for making weapons."

Man-at-Arms stood up and waved, and a crowd of dwarfs poured out from among the rocks and surrounded the wind raider.

Laughing and chattering to each other the dwarfs gathered round the Masters of the Universe.

A slightly taller dwarf stepped forward, and Man-at-Arms cried, "Trog, my old friend! That was a fine load of metal you sent me last time."

"We dig nothing but the finest," replied Trog. "Who are your companions and what are you doing in these parts?"

Quickly Man-at-Arms explained who He-Man and Teela were. Then he told Trog, who was leader of the dwarfs, about their rescue bid.

The dwarfs looked at one another. "The Vale of Caldor is an evil place," they said. "We avoid it if we can. But if you *must* go there, we will be your guides. Our mines and tunnels pass under the mountains. There you will be invisible even to the evil magic of Skeletor until you reach the Vale itself."

He-Man piloted the wind raider into hiding among the rocks, where a dwarf stood guard over it. Then, led by dwarfs carrying torches, He-Man, Teela and Man-at-Arms set off into the heart of the Ice Mountains.

19

Through the twisting, winding tunnels the
dwarfs led He-Man, Teela and Man-at-Arms. In
places the rocky roof was so low that even the
dwarfs had to stoop to pass. In others the
tunnels opened out into caverns whose roofs
were so high that the light of the torches failed
to reach them.

At length the level passage began to slope steeply upwards. When it was almost too steep to walk, the party found themselves climbing a staircase cut in the rock.

As they paused to rest at the top of a flight of steps they could hear a distant sound of water. And in a few moments their path took them across a stone arch over a swift underground river. The river flowed into a lake, and at the far end of the lake a mighty waterfall tumbled out of the darkness above with a loud roar.

They left the lake, and were just approaching a tunnel entrance when, without warning, a screaming mass of dark shapes sprang out of the shadows.

"TROLLS!" cried Trog.

The trolls outnumbered the dwarfs many times. Their sharp claws caught the light from the torches, and their fangs were bared in blood lust. Quickly Trog ordered the dwarfs into a line. Then they drew swords and swung axes as they faced the trolls.

He-Man watched for a moment. The trolls had not yet noticed the full-sized figures in the dim light. He-Man, Teela and Man-at-Arms aimed their energy weapons and He-Man cried, "Trog, order your men to fall back."

The line of dwarfs divided in two. The trolls found themselves face to face with three armed humans twice the size of the dwarfs. For a moment they stopped.

He-Man gave a signal, and bolts of energy blasted from the Masters' weapons. The trolls were bowled over in all directions. They fought one another as they tried to escape. The Masters ceased firing, and the dwarfs charged. Soon there was not a troll to be seen.

The sound of the last fleeing troll died in the distance. Trog led the way once more, and in a short time daylight appeared in front of them. A few more steps and the party came out of the tunnel. They found themselves on a broad ledge high above a deep valley. "There," said Trog, "is the Vale of Caldor."

In the centre of a bubbling, fuming lake was a small island. He-Man held Stratos' ring at arm's length towards the island. The stone glowed faintly. "Delora is somewhere on the

24

island," he said. "But there is no way to reach her without the wind raider. With my weight alone it should be possible to cross over the mountains."

Escorted by the dwarfs, He-Man set off back through the tunnels.

There was no sign of the trolls, but as they crossed the rock arch they found the way barred by the figure of a strange-looking warrior. "A gnoll," exclaimed He-Man. He drew his weapon. The gnoll charged, but one blast from He-Man and it stumbled back in panic, lost its footing, and fell with a loud splash into the river far below.

Back at the wind raider, He-Man lost no time
in checking the power system. Then he climbed
behind the controls. With a wave to the dwarfs
he set the powerful machine at maximum ascent
and roared upwards towards the snowy peaks.
Swiftly the wind raider gained height, skimming
just clear of the side of the mountains. Despite
the craft's heating system, the icy cold of the
mountains chilled He-Man's hands on the
controls. Frost and icicles formed on the outside
surfaces.

The air grew thinner the higher He-Man flew.
Freezing winds buffeted the machine. Then the
snow clouds closed in. He-Man now only
occasionally had a glimpse of the mountainside.
Then through a gap in the cloud he saw a sharp
peak directly in front. A last sharp burst of
power and the wind raider was over the summit
and diving into the Vale of Caldor.

Below, on their ledge, Teela and Man-at-
Arms heard the roar of the wind raider's jets as
He-Man tried to locate his companions through
the thick cloud.

Quickly Teela held her Kobra power sceptre
above her head and sent out a powerful energy
beam. In the wind raider He-Man saw his
energy blade pulse with power. Steering round
until the pulses were strongest he dropped down
to land beside Teela.

In his lair inside Snake Mountain, Skeletor
had his slaves bring Stratos before him. "You
poor fool," he gloated. "Did you really think
that giving yourself up would do any good?
While I decide your fate you shall join me in
watching the feeble antics of your friends."

The Lord of Destruction pressed a switch and
part of the rock wall slid aside to reveal a huge
video screen. Another touch to the controls and
there before them lay the Vale of Caldor.

In the centre of the boiling lake lay the island. And on the island was a small figure.

"DELORA!" cried Stratos.

"And here we have your noble friends who hope to rescue her," mocked Skeletor. And Stratos saw He-Man, Teela and Man-at-Arms clustered around the wind raider as they planned what to do next.

He-Man scanned the cliffs surrounding the lake. Wyverns perched on every crag. Their wings were folded. But their eyes never blinked as they stood guard over the lake, the island, and the prisoner. Only on the ledge high on the mountain were the Masters of the Universe out of their sight.

"These monsters make things difficult," said He-Man. "Before the wind raider was halfway to the island the nearest wyvern could seize Delora and carry her off again."

"Could we not try after dark?" suggested Teela.

"Wyverns see as well in the dark as in daylight," replied He-Man.

"Then, we will make our own dark," said Man-at-Arms. "With the help of the snow and a little work on the wind raider we will blind these evil creatures long enough to carry out our task."

Using the tool kit from the wind raider, Man-at-Arms set to work.

Man-at-Arms' skill made short work of his
task. Then He-Man took the controls and the
wind raider lifted off with a roar of its jets. Up
went the powerful craft until it was level with
the great snow cornices which overhung the lake
far below.

Skimming just above the snow, He-Man
pressed the extra control fitted by Man-at-Arms.
Instantly the jets sent a blast of super-heat down
on to the snow. The snow melted, and all round
the valley it began to slip and slide in a vast

avalanche into the boiling lake. In a moment
clouds of dense steam rose into the air, filling
the valley and covering the island.

Instantly, He-Man put the wind raider into a
steep dive. Stratos' ring was glowing. Now it
began to flash, brighter and faster every
moment. Through the haze He-Man made out
the shape of the island. As the wind raider came
down on the shore, Delora ran down from
among the rocks and leapt aboard.

The last of the snow fell into the lake and the steam began to lift. Almost touching the bubbling surface, the wind raider skimmed low at top speed. The way ahead was clear, but above was still covered in a thick layer of steam.

The guarding wyverns heard the sound of the jets, but even their keen sight was helpless to see anything. Several of the fierce reptiles dived from their perches after the invisible enemy. They tried to follow the echoes of the

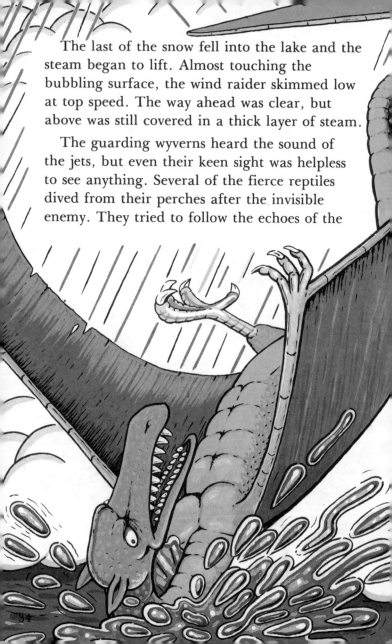

wind raider's engines. Screeching with rage they flew blindly about. Some crashed into the mountainside. Others collided with each other. And two, in head-on collision, fell into the boiling waters of the lake.

Again guided by Teela's Kobra sceptre, He-Man brought the wind raider in to land on the ledge. Trog and the dwarfs were waiting. While He-Man took off on the return journey over the mountain, they escorted Teela, Man-at-Arms and Delora back through the tunnels.

On the video screen Skeletor watched as the steam cloud obscured the picture. Angrily he moved the controls, but the image was no clearer. He had an occasional glimpse of a baffled wyvern, but that was all. He guessed that his prisoner had escaped.

With a scream of rage, the Lord of Destruction crashed his fist on the control panel. "I am served by fools and weaklings," he roared, and sent a blast from his Havoc staff crackling across the cavern.

In a panic his slaves scurried for cover, leaving Stratos unguarded. Dodging another blast, the Lord of the Air soared up to the cavern roof. Skeletor fired again, but only succeeded in bringing down a section of rock.

"Careful!" mocked Stratos. "Even the Lord of Destruction needs a roof over his head!"

Through the passages and caverns inside
Snake Mountain, Stratos led the raging Skeletor.
Skeletor tried every trick he knew, but Stratos'
aerobatics left him panting and bewildered.

Every part of Skeletor's lair contained cunning
traps. These were meant to stop enemies getting
in, or getting out. But Stratos evaded them all.

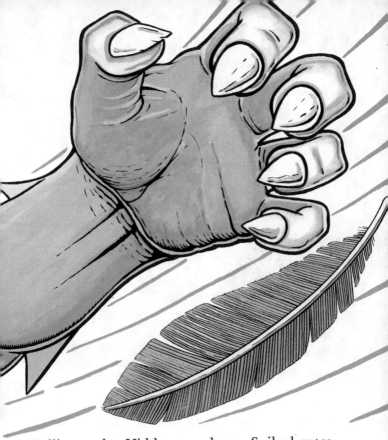

Falling rocks. Hidden trapdoors. Spiked gates. Stratos swooped and circled, just out of reach. Now, they were at the entrance to the mountain lair.

Daylight shone outside the gloomy gateway. But, instead of making his escape, Stratos kept on taunting Skeletor, drawing him always closer to the archway.

Skeletor's eyes blazed red in his bony skull. Mad with rage he watched Stratos skim through the gate to the bridge linking the twin peaks of Snake Mountain.

The Lord of the Air came down on the bridge. But as he did so he gave a cry of pain and collapsed, clutching his leg.

Skeletor gave a great cry of triumph. "Let that be a lesson to you! You thought that you could outwit and make a fool of Skeletor, Lord of Destruction! You are at my mercy!" And he strode through the gate towards the fallen Stratos.

Too late, he realised that he had been tricked. The trapdoor which guarded the entrance to Snake Mountain crashed open. With a scream, Skeletor plunged into a deep and foul dungeon.

"Goodbye!" cried Stratos. "I think it will be many hours before your frightened slaves come to get you out!"

At Castle Grayskull He-Man, Teela and Man-at-Arms waited with Delora. Before long Stratos joined them and described how he had tricked Skeletor into falling foul of one of his own traps.

He-Man returned Stratos' ring as Delora and her husband prepared to return to their mountain home in the fair land of Avion.

When they had gone, He-Man stood alone on the battlements. He heard the sound of wings. It was the great falcon Zoar. The noble bird circled the castle and perched on a pinnacle close to He-Man. The bird's dark eyes glowed and in his mind He-Man heard the voice of the Sorceress.

"You have done well, and have used your power wisely. But, remember, without the aid of Trog and his people, things might have been very different. Never forget that even the smallest of the people of Eternia have a part to play in overcoming the powers of evil."

Then the bird was gone, and He-Man prepared to return to the palace and his other life as the gentle Prince Adam.